"YOU CAN'T HURT US,
WE'RE TOUGH."

"That howl didn't sound like you were tough. It sounded like you were hurt. Should I call my mother over here?"

"No, let's just play. Tag, you're it!" Snow bumped me on the side.

"That's not fair." I pouted.

"Anything is fair in tag. Come get me." Snow's blue eyes stared straight at me.

I charged at him and missed. Stretching my legs, I pretended to flip my ears at a fly. Instantly I darted toward him. "Got you, Snow!"

"That's good, Bub! You get better every time." Snow crouched on the ground with his head low and his ears perked. Blue eyes narrowed as he stared at me.

That's when I saw them. Looming behind Snow were five huge creatures with their teeth bared. A low-pitched growl came from one of the enormous beasts. I backed up a step, just as Snow leaped at me.

Suddenly we were both falling and sliding at the same time. Tumbling, Snow and I scraped and bumped as we fell over the edge of the cliff.

Books by Bill Wallace:

The Backward Bird Dog
Beauty
The Biggest Klutz in Fifth Grade
Blackwater Swamp
Buffalo Gal
The Christmas Spurs
Coyote Autumn
Danger in Quicksand Swamp
Danger on Panther Peak
  [*Original title*: Shadow on the
  Snow]
A Dog Called Kitty
Eye of the Great Bear
Ferret in the Bedroom, Lizards
  in the Fridge
The Final Freedom
Journey into Terror
Never Say Quit
Red Dog
Snot Stew
Totally Disgusting!
Trapped in Death Cave
True Friends
Upchuck and the Rotten Willy
Upchuck and the Rotten Willy:
  The Great Escape
Upchuck and the Rotten Willy:
  Running Wild
Watchdog and the Coyotes

Books by Carol and Bill Wallace:

The Flying Flea, Callie, and Me
That Furball Puppy and Me
Chomps, Flea, and Gray Cat
  (That's Me!)
Bub Moose
Bub, Snow and the Burly Bear
  Scare

Books by Nikki Wallace:

Stubby and the Puppy Pack
Stubby and the Puppy Pack to
  the Rescue

Available from Simon & Schuster

Carol Wallace and Bill Wallace

Bub Moose

Illustrated by John Steven Gurney

Aladdin Paperbacks
New York London Toronto Sydney Singapore

First Aladdin Paperbacks edition October 2002

Text copyright © 2001 by Bill Wallace and Carol Wallace
Interior illustrations copyright © 2001 by John Steven Gurney

ALADDIN PAPERBACKS
An imprint of Simon & Schuster
Children's Publishing Division
1230 Avenue of the Americas
New York, NY 10020

Also available in a Minstrel Books hardcover edition.
Printed in the United States of America
10 9 8 7 6 5 4 3 2

Library of Congress Catalog Card Number: 2001098831
ISBN: 0-7434-0639-7 (Aladdin pbk.)

To the "real" Bub Moose—
You know who you are!
and
To Jane Johnston,
Who's been waiting!

Bub Moose

Chapter 1

Something rubbed against me. In one way it felt good. In another it was rough. At least I guess it was. I didn't know for sure because I hadn't felt much before. I do remember that I was warm and safe and cozy. The only sound was the steady *thump-thump, thump-thump, thump-thump.*

Then suddenly everything got light. Even with my eyes closed, the brightness hurt. I was no longer surrounded by a feeling of warmth and comfort. Instead, it became cold and a little scary. The steady *thump-thump* was replaced by all sorts of strange and frightening noises.

Something touched me. It was warm and damp. It went over my whole body until I was dry and comfortable.

"Open your eyes, my baby." The voice was soft

and gentle. "Listen to your mother and open your eyes. It's time to see your new world."

Something pushed me so hard I almost tipped over. I tilted, then stretched out my front feet. Quickly I pulled my body up. My back legs were wobbly. I tried to balance, but fell into the warm bed of grass where I had been born. Mother was close. I could feel her presence, but when I tried to look at her, the light hurt my eyes. She pushed at me again.

"You have to get up," Mother warned. "The quicker you get on your feet, the safer you will be."

I opened my eyes as wide as I could. My mother was the most beautiful thing I had ever seen. She had a big furry nose that was soft as could be. Her head and face were almost as long as I was. Her large ears twitched to chase away the tiny little black things that buzzed around her head.

"This feels good. I want to stay here." I flipped my ears and tried to flatten myself into the big nest.

"Come on, it's time to move. We are safe here, but you need to get on your feet!" Mother shoved me again with her beautiful soft nose.

I stretched my legs out. Everything felt wobbly again. I put my weight on my front feet, then my back feet. No matter how much I balanced or which way I moved, I couldn't stay up. Then *thud*, I was back on the ground.

Okay, I'll try again. Shoving my front legs out, I lifted my bottom up. Just before my back legs were steady, my front legs collapsed back into the warm nest.

"Let me rest a bit," I said as I shut my eyes.

"You have to get up and move around. The longer you wait, the more danger you are in." Mother shoved at my back end.

Move, legs. I tried to straighten my front ones again. They didn't want to cooperate. *Okay. One leg. Move!*

One leg slowly stretched out straight. Both front hooves were in the right position. I tried to jerk my body up. My legs didn't seem to be part of me.

I tried shoving my hooves out and pushing my rear end up at the same time. *Yeah! It's working!*

Blap! I hit the ground again. Something must be wrong.

I could feel Mother's big nose lifting my rear. My front hooves suddenly slipped straight out in front of me and my bottom rose up. My hind legs straightened at just the right time to balance my body. I was up. I tried to move each leg one at a time. My front ones were steady, as I took small steps toward Mother. I tried to tell my rear end to come along, too. It didn't listen. I felt wobbly, trying to make everything work together. All at once I found myself back on the ground. *This is useless. I need to rest.*

"Try again, little one, you can make it." Mother nudged me.

One more time I stretched out my front legs and pulled up with all of my strength. Now all four legs felt weird. I shook my body carefully as I balanced myself. Mother's soft brown eyes gave me courage.

"Let's go, baby. I know you can do it."

Carefully I made small steps with my front hooves. My back legs felt stronger as I moved them forward, too. Each small step made me feel more sturdy. I shook my whole body again. I didn't fall down!

"Hey, this is fun." I tried to bounce just a bit.

I toppled over. *Back on the ground again.*

"Okay. I'm ready this time. Help me just a little."

Mother gave me a soft nudge. "I think you are strong enough now, small one. Let's go!"

With one big push I was up. All of my legs worked at the same time. My body balanced over them. I was standing. My front feet popped up off the ground, but not very high.

Mother licked my fur again. It almost threw me off balance, but I managed to catch myself. *Hey, I can handle this,* I thought.

Mother lifted her head. She seemed very proud. "You can hop and jump soon. Right now you need to practice balancing and walking."

Mother pulled me toward her with her chin. She didn't tell me what to do. She didn't have to. I was really hungry! Something inside of me knew exactly where to go.

After dinner I felt stronger than ever. Then slowly we started walking.

"What are these?" I asked, sniffing the long pointy things beneath my feet.

"Those are pine needles," Mother answered.

"What's that?"

"A leaf."

"Where do they come from?"

"We live in a forest," Mother said patiently. "The pine needles and leaves come from the trees that shelter us. See up there."

I raised my head to look up. I guess I shouldn't have. My back feet must have been too close to my front feet because when I raised my head I toppled backward. I landed with a thud.

"Oops," I stammered.

Mother smiled. "It's okay. Now hop up and let's go."

"Wait, what's all that bright shiny stuff up there?"

"Up where?"

"Above the trees with all the pine needles and leaves on them."

"That's the sky," Mother answered. "The sky is blue and the leaves are green and the trees are brown."

I felt my eyes roll. *This is a lot to remember.*

I took a step but almost fell again when my hoof tripped over something.

"That's a really big leaf," I gasped.

"That's a limb," Mother corrected. "Limbs are brown like the trees. They fall to the forest floor sometimes, too."

I felt my head hang low when I sighed.

"There's so much to see and to remember. I'll never get it all straight."

Mother's soft brown eyes seemed to twinkle. She licked me with her warm tongue. "It just takes time," she said. "You haven't even been here an hour yet. You're doing very well."

A loud *tap-tap-tap* made my ear twitch and turn toward the sound. Mama looked down at me.

"Listen. Do you hear that sound?" she asked.

Both my ears perked in the direction where I heard the noise. The loud tapping came from a tree above us.

"What is it?" I stretched my neck to see better. This time I didn't fall on my bottom.

"That's a woodpecker. When you hear her tapping, that means you are safe. When she is quiet, you need to be very alert for danger."

I stepped over logs and limbs without getting my legs tangled up. I followed Mother farther into the trees. I couldn't see her pretty face when I was behind her. All I could see were her long legs. I stayed close enough to touch them every now and then with my nose. Being close to Mother made me feel safe.

"Where are we going? I want to go back home." I was getting tired.

"You are home. The whole forest is our home. As long as you listen and watch carefully, you are safe here. You have to know the danger sounds and the safe places to go when something isn't right." Mother turned around. Her big nose grazed my neck. She gently blew warm air against me. I felt safe and secure.

"You do need to choose a name. We have to decide what we are going to call you. That is one of the first things a baby moose must do." Mother nuzzled me again.

"How do I choose? I just got here. How can I pick a name?" I looked up into Mother's big brown eyes.

"It's important that your name fits you. That it is something you recognize and feel good about." Mother let out a snort. "Stay here in the tall grass. You can think about it a little more while I get some nice soft pond weeds."

I lay down, as I was told. When Mother started to walk away, I tried to struggle to my feet.

"You're not leaving me, are you?"

"I'll be very close. You can see me in the water over there." Mother was calm as she slowly walked away.

Folding my legs, I nestled into the soft grass. Mother walked quietly into the pond. I watched as she moved through the water. Suddenly she disappeared. I stretched my neck trying to see her. All that was left was the swirling water where she had disappeared. I felt very alone. Then Mother's bottom popped up above the surface. I tilted my head to one side. *She must be eating something under the water,* I thought. As I started to go help her, she raised her head and looked at me. Water poured from her chin and cheeks. A long strand of grass hung from her mouth.

While I lay quietly, Mother continued to drop into the water, looking for tender bits of pond weed. Her bottom would pop to the surface, then her head would follow. I worried about her at first, then I knew that she was okay.

I rested my head on my front legs. Closing my eyes, I listened to the sounds of the forest. I knew that I must become familiar with each noise in my new home.

As days went by I found that my mother was right. Just as she had told me, I began to learn the calls of many forest birds. The little things that buzzed around our heads were bugs. Mother called them flies. Sometimes they were hungry. When they bit my ears, it hurt—but not too bad. Other times they tickled when they landed in my fur. Mostly, except for the buzzing sounds, I never even noticed them. There were other bugs in the grass and weeds. They all made different sounds and did different things. Mother was right. I was learning a lot. Still . . .

The name thing really bothered me.

Chapter 2

"Stay here, little one. I'm going into the pond, and you're not quite ready for that. Besides, you need to think of a name."

I watched as Mother sloshed into the water. Settling down into the soft leaves and twigs, I rested my chin on my front legs. A small butterfly landed on my ear. It tickled. I twitched carefully. She flittered by my face and landed on a log nearby. I watched her without moving so much as an eyelash. The butterfly stretched out her wings, then fluttered away. She moved along with the gentle breeze. Thinking up a name needed lots of concentration. My eyes closed.

A name. I need a name. This is harder than learning to walk.

Tap! Tap! The woodpecker's noises made me feel safe and comfortable.

"Buzz, shirrr, zoom . . ." The bugs in the forest sounded loud against the quiet of the trees.

Opening my eyes, I could see a few of the tiny things creeping slowly around the grass and weeds. Their small movements were magnified when I concentrated on each one. Very still—without the slightest wiggle—I tried to spot as many as I could. I counted and counted, then closed my eyes again. *I have to think of a name.*

I was almost asleep when a new sound came to my ears. It was almost like the noise the birds made when they were scratching in the ground, looking for food. Still, it was louder . . . bigger, somehow. I didn't move a muscle. Slowly I opened my eyes. I couldn't see a thing.

"Hey, Bub! Hey . . . Pay attention!"

"What?" I gasped. I jumped up and spun around.

The voice wasn't sweet and soft like Mother's. It was rough, like someone with rocks in his throat. Next a harsh scraping sound came to my ears.

"I said, 'Hey, Bub! Pay attention!'"

No, this wasn't Mother's sweet sound. It wasn't friendly at all. The voice was deep and gruff. I stared at the spot where it came from. All that I could see was a tree. It looked funny. Not like the others in the forest. It was big at the bottom, but in the middle it was narrow and white. The top was like other trees. It didn't have very many leaves, though.

"I didn't know that trees could talk!"

"What's wrong with you, Bub? I'm not a tree. Listen to me. You need to pay attention, or you're going to get hurt!"

"What does pay attention mean? I know how to listen." I suddenly had that alone feeling again.

"Pay attention means watch what you're doing. Right now you need to look out!"

"Look out for what?" I strained my eyes trying to find out who was talking to me.

"You're not very bright are you, Bub?" The gravelly voice seemed close.

"I'm smart enough. I just haven't been here very long. Why don't you show me where you are?"

"Are you crazy? I don't want to get hit in the head. You need to wake up and pay attention!"

"Pay attention to WHAT?"

Suddenly a brown face poked out from behind the tree. Two large yellow teeth stuck out from the face. "Look out for *this,* you twit!"

"For what?" I asked again.

"The tree, you silly little thing. It's going to fall, and you're right in the way."

Looking up, I noticed the tall thin tree swaying back and forth in the breeze.

I jumped away as fast as my legs would let me. I ran toward the pond and Mother.

"Cra-a-ack!" The sound was new to my ears. The smell of fresh wood came to my nose. I glanced back over my shoulder to see what had happened.

The tall tree tilted way to one side. Slowly it fell toward the ground. *Smack!* The thing landed just inches from the spot where I had been sleeping.

"Hey, what was that? How did you do that?" Moving closer, I sniffed at the tree that lay still and quiet on the ground.

"It's easy, Bub. That's what beavers do all day."

"You're a beaver? Where do you live? I haven't seen you before." Stepping closer for a better look, I tried to check him out.

"My whole family is over there in the pond. We have to work hard all day to keep our lodge safe. Then, there's the dam to repair so the water doesn't leak out and food to gather for winter and . . ." He sighed. "Just so much work for a beaver, and so little time."

I looked toward the pond. Mother popped up, but she didn't come to my rescue. I guess she hadn't heard the crash. The beaver gnawed and tore at the small limbs on the tree that he had sent to the ground.

"How many are in your family?" I asked. "We just have Mother and me in our family." I dropped my head and perked my ears toward the tree.

"Hey, Bub, I don't have time for chitchat! I've got work to do."

"Sorry. I'm just curious. Mother says baby moose are supposed to be curious. I don't mean to bother you, but I was resting comfortably and *you* almost dropped a tree right on me!" I shook my body. The memory of the tree landing where I had been sleeping gave me the shivers.

"That's not my problem. Your mother should have put you in a safer place. This forest belongs to me and my family. Move along, I've got work to do!"

"You tried to flatten me with a tree! I want to know more about you so that I can watch out for you and your family." I peered down my nose at him.

"Get lost, Bub! I don't have time. Your mother should have told you about us already." I watched as the beaver cut limbs with his sharp yellow teeth, then pulled them away.

Watching him, I lay down in the grass. The animal was covered with brown fur, the kind I had seen on other animals. Yet he was *different*. Instead of a nice fluffy tail, his looked like a piece of wood. Or maybe a pinecone, only flat. He had a big head and his jaws had to be very strong. The limbs seemed to fly off the tree.

"Why are your ears so small?" I tried to look at my own big floppy ears. Mother had beautiful large ears.

"Eh . . . You still here, Bub? Don't you get it? I want you to get lost!"

"I don't want to get lost. Mother would be lonely without me. What's your name?"

The beaver squinted his eyes and looked my way. "Good grief, don't you ever give up? You're a question a minute."

"How can I learn anything if I don't ask questions? What's your name?"

The beaver turned away from the log and sat down. The big hump on his back made him look huge. I stretched my neck to get a closer look. His big flat tail stretched out behind him. It gave a little thump on the ground.

"Dudley. They call me Dudley. Any more questions?" He squinted his eyes tightly.

"That's a nice name. Why do you squint your eyes?"

"Hey, Bub, I was just kidding. I don't *really* need more questions!" His tiny ears twitched a little.

"As soon as I know everything about you, I won't *ever* have to ask you another question. So this is just going to save you time." That made sense. At least to me.

"You think so, Bub? I have work to do, but give it a go." Dudley leaned against the tree that he had dropped to the ground.

"First question?"

"Why are you squinting at me? Your eyes don't look very big. My eyes are big and round. You smush your eyes tight. How can you see?"

"That's more than one question. I knew that you couldn't pay attention. I'll say it again. First question."

"Okay, why do you squint?"

"That's very good. Actually, I can't see very well. I have to count on my hearing and my sense of smell to tell me what's going on. I could smell you, and I could tell you weren't dangerous, so I decided to warn you. Usually, when a tree starts to fall, I have to run like crazy to make sure it doesn't land on me. This was just your lucky day. Now, I have to get busy."

"Wait! Just one more question, please." I scooted even closer to the beaver.

"Okay, but remember you have to pay attention. Question two?" He closed his eyes. He smushed his face up tight. His big yellow teeth seemed to shine in the light that came through the trees.

"Why do you have a tail like that? It should be fluffy like your body."

"What are you talking about, Bub? I've got THE BEST tail in the whole forest. It helps me swim. It helps me warn my family. I can slap the water so they know there's danger. You need to pay attention! Besides, if you look close, you can see that there are some hairs on my tail. Not many, I guess. You should have a good tail like mine. I need to get busy. You have any more questions, go ask your mother. She knows us. She pays attention. When there is trouble around the pond, she listens for our warnings. Go back to sleep. Moose need their rest. This beaver has work to do, Bub!" He turned back toward the tree.

Lying down and tucking my body into a ball, I listened to the forest sounds. I could hear the soft crunch of Dudley gnawing on the tree. Birds chirped above me. Insects buzzed and whizzed around in the grass. Mother would be here soon.

When I woke up, Mother was pushing me with her big nose. "Let's go, baby. You don't look like you've been thinking of a name."

"Uhh . . . uhhh . . . Sure I have. It's Bub!" I smiled. "Bub Moose!"

Chapter 3

Well, it's Bub, is it? Did you get some help with that?" My mother's big eyes seemed to shine brighter.

"I got a little help, I guess. Well, it was Dudley over there." I turned my head toward the tree where the big beaver was still working.

"Oh, Dudley helped you? The two of you did very well. I'm glad that you finally decided on a name." Mother nudged at me with her nose.

"Dudley said that you knew all about his family. Does he have a big family? Do they all live in the pond?"

"Beavers have lived in the forest a long time. Dudley and his mate were already here when I came. Twelve is the most that I have seen in the pond. They call the babies *kits*. They stay with their parents for two years, then they have to find new homes for themselves. It would be too crowded if they all stayed here, so the young ones move on. Dudley teaches them well. They know how to find food and protect themselves when they leave."

"Where is the rest of *our* family?" I looked up at Mother.

"You and I are family, little Bub Moose!" Mother licked at my fur.

"Is that all the family that we have? You said there were lots of beavers in the pond. Dudley said that was his family." I stretched my neck to get a bite of leaves from a bush nearby.

"Well, your father is in the woods. Moose usually browse alone. You also have an older sister who has gone out in the forest by herself. Someday you will be ready to go out on your own. Right now, you just need to learn how to take care of yourself. There are many lessons for a young moose to learn." Mother pushed me toward the pond.

"I'm a good learner. There are just some questions I have to ask to be sure." Walking to the edge of the pond, I slowly followed Mother into the water. She must have thought I was ready for the pond now that I had a name. I could feel the dampness on my legs and stomach. I sucked up a big drink. Mother stepped farther away.

"What do you find to eat in here?" I shook my face in the cool water.

"The tender pond weeds along the bottom are good for moose. Sometimes we have to dive down a ways to get to them, but they are wonderful. Follow me. We'll explore the pond a bit." I stayed close behind Mother as she waded deeper into the water.

"Put your head down, Bub Moose. The roots are under the surface, way down near the mud.

"Won't I get water in my nose?"

Mama shook her head. "No. We moose have very special noses. It keeps water from coming in. All you have to do is take a deep breath before going under, and your nose will take care of the rest."

I took a deep breath and did what she told me. It was scary, but Mother was right. My nose didn't let any water inside at all.

Mother smiled when I raised my head. Little drops poured from my face and chin. Mother kissed my ear with her long pink tongue.

"See, that wasn't too bad. With a little practice, you can stay under the water for a long time. You can remain long enough to gather as much food as you want."

I peered down. Things became clearer as I moved my body deeper into the water. Lots of small weeds poked up from the bottom. I liked the way the tender shoots felt in my mouth.

When I looked up, Mother was still by my side. "Good work, Bub Moose. You are such a

quick learner. Do you want to go deeper into the pond?"

Mother nudged me gently, and we walked farther away from the bank. As the water flowed higher around my body, I felt lighter on my feet. I could bob and float. My legs pumped and I could move around without even touching the bottom. Keeping my head high, I watched Mother as I practiced swimming.

"That is enough for today." Mother moved back toward the shore.

"But I like this. It feels good. Let me stay a little longer." I bobbed a few more times. The look on Mother's face helped me decide to follow her to shore.

"You will have lots of time to practice swimming, Bub Moose. Right now we need to find a place to rest for the night. You are getting stronger, and before long I won't have to worry about your safety. Right now, though, we need to think about a place to sleep."

We walked awhile before Mother helped me nestle down in some pine needles. She finally settled down, too. Her big ears stayed perked as she listened to the new sounds the night was bringing.

"There are lots of things in the world that you need to know. One day you will have big antlers on your head to help protect yourself."

"What is an antler? How will I get one?"

"As you grow, so will your antlers. They are like strong trees on your head. They help you push your way through the forest. You will use them to protect yourself from big animals that try to hurt you. Your father has antlers. Later in the year we will be able to see them shining in the sunlight. We will watch for him near the pond. When winter gets close, his antlers fall to the ground. In spring they start to grow again."

I nestled against Mother's soft brown fur. "Do I need to be afraid of anything else?"

"I can protect you from almost everything now, little Bub Moose. Each day you are growing stronger, and soon you will be able to protect yourself. You just have to pay attention to the things that are around you." Mother licked my fur again.

"Pay attention! That is what Dudley said. He said that I *didn't* pay attention. What do I need to do?" I tried to flatten myself lower into the needles.

"As you get bigger, you must listen and watch for everything that happens in the forest. Keep your ears alert to all that goes on around you. Before you move, take time to watch. Go carefully from place to place. When you are young, there are lots of dangers in the forest. But when you are grown—when you are strong and tall and handsome, like your father—there is hardly anything that will frighten you."

I closed my eyes and tried to think what Father

looked like. He must be big like Mother. He had trees coming out of his head. I let out a little snort at what that must look like.

"Bub Moose, keep your ears perked and listen to the forest sounds. Do you hear anything unusual?" Mother's big ears turned toward the valley.

I tried to perk my ears like Mother's. I listened as carefully as I could. Sounds came to my ears—noises that I had not heard before. A steady roar came from the trees in the distance. Then from nowhere a howling noise seemed to surround us. I looked at Mother. Her ears were still and pointed. I watched her as she quietly stood up. Her huge body seemed to hover over me as the howling slowly moved away from us.

"I wanted you to hear the noises from the cars on the road. They are the most dangerous things for us. We have to watch for them and the people that they bring." Mother gently settled her big body back down into the nest that we had made.

"What was that other sound? It was so near." I nestled closer to Mother's warmth.

"Wolves. They make a lot of noise, but they really aren't much danger to us. I can protect you from them. In a few months you will be able to take care of yourself against a wolf. People . . . they are something else. You can never be safe from them. Most of them are okay, but some come to the forest to harm us. Cars that bring people here are always a danger.

They move fast. All animals have to be watchful of them. Look over there. Can you see the shiny spots? Those are lights from a car. You must stay away from those places, especially at night."

The twinkling lights moved briskly before my eyes. They looked like the stars in the sky, only they moved so quickly.

"Can we go see them sometime?"

"Yes, sometime. But we can only go in the daylight, Bub Moose. People whiz by so fast that most times they don't see us very well even when the sun is shining. Nighttime is more dangerous. There are places where we can see people who aren't in their cars. People are interesting. They walk around on two legs instead of four. They slosh around the swamps, but they have trouble spotting us. We can see them. Their colors are bright and they show up against the trees and brush."

I closed my eyes and tried to imagine what people were. Father must look like Mother, but people . . . with bright colors . . . shiny lights . . . I didn't know.

"Can we go see people and their cars? I will pay attention. I will follow all of my lessons. Please, can we go?" I looked at Mother. Her ears were still perked as she stared into the darkness.

"Bub Moose, you are a good little moose. You have been learning your lessons very well. I am proud of you. Tomorrow, in the daylight, we will go down to the people place. This is a safe time of the year. We will have to stay away from their cars, though. Can you do that?"

"I'll pay attention, Mother. I will listen to you very carefully." Closing my eyes, I tried to rest. Bright colors and shiny lights were visions in my head that wouldn't let me go to sleep. I wiggled and twisted.

"Bub Moose, it's time for bed. If you are going to take a long walk with me tomorrow, you need your rest." Mother put her head against me.

"I will, Mother. I'll pay attention." I thought about the things that Mother had told me. Each time I closed my eyes something new would pop into my head.

Chapter 4

I knew that I needed to rest up for the trip, but it was hard to go to sleep. When I wiggled, Mother nudged me gently with her beautiful nose. I tried to listen for the peaceful sounds of the night forest. Owl called out a loud "Whoo!" Tilting my ears, I heard another "whoo" in the distance. Owl's wings were so quiet that only the keenest ears, like mine, could hear as he whooshed near our nest and moved on. I was awake most of the night listening for familiar sounds.

When the light finally broke, I opened my eyes. Mother wasn't there!

"Mother!" Fear tightened around me.

Near the pond I heard a loud "Hronk!"

Frantically I scrambled to my feet and hurried to

her. Nuzzling her side, I started my breakfast. I felt warm and safe.

Mother continued to browse. When I finished eating, I took a few leaps into the air. Stretching my legs and bouncing as high as I could, I started running around the clearing. I was ready to go, but I had to be patient. Maybe running would help.

Keeping a close eye on Mother, I moved slowly toward the pond. Maybe I could find Dudley. The sticky mud clung to my feet as I searched for signs of the beaver.

Spotting movement near the edge of the water, I stepped closer. My eyes narrowed. Keeping my head low, I watched, trying to figure out what it was. Suddenly birds fluttered up. They startled me and made me jump. Only, I didn't go anyplace. My feet were stuck in the gooey mud. They skidded and slipped, but I couldn't move from my spot. Confused and a little scared, I started to run. Only instead of running, all I managed to do was splash mud all over the place.

"Hey, Bub!" A familiar voice seemed to pierce the air.

"What?" My feet were still sticky and out of control.

"Slow down, Bub. You're making a big mess out of my pond."

"I'm stuck and you're worried about YOUR pond!" My legs shook as I tried to pull them loose.

"Hey, Bub! Calm down. Real moose don't get stuck in anything! Take your time. Cool off a minute!" Dudley's voice soothed my shaky legs.

"What do I do?"

"Take just a few seconds and look all around. Are there any limbs against your feet?"

I stared at the gooey stuff that was holding me. "I don't see anything except MUD!"

"Okay then, slowly pull your back feet out carefully, one at a time."

I pulled my hind legs from the sticky hold. My front legs came out easily, too.

"Thanks, Dudley. You saved my life."

"Don't worry about it, Bub. You just have to pay attention." Dudley went back chopping trees.

"Hronk, hronk!" At last Mother was ready to go.

"Remember your lessons, Bub Moose. You have to stay close and listen to everything that I tell you. There is always danger when we get near people, and you have to be ready." Mother nudged my side.

"I will be ready." I promised.

"Then follow close behind me. Watch your step and keep your eyes open."

I stayed right behind Mother as we followed trails that took us to the bottom of the mountain.

"Mother, I see a stream. Can we get a drink?"

"Pay attention, Bub Moose. Look carefully!" Mother stared at the place where the water was.

Frowning, I stared at it as well. It looked like water. It shone and sparkled in the sun, only it didn't seem to move. There was a long yellow stripe in the middle of it, too.

"Listen, Bub Moose. Do you hear anything strange?"

Perking my ears like Mother's, I tried to recognize the new sound that roared closer. I looked up at Mother's face. She didn't look frightened, so I wouldn't be afraid, either.

I watched the spot where the sound came from. It grew louder and louder. Suddenly a huge monster came toward us. It stayed on the place that I thought was water. I had never seen anything so ugly in my life. It was big. No, it was huge! The gray monster raced past the spot where we stood. But it didn't run on legs like we had. Its legs were big and black and round. They spun so fast I couldn't even see its hooves. The horrible sound grew quieter.

As we stood in the clearing, smaller monsters followed the same path that the big monster had taken. A few came from the other direction. The monsters, all different colors and shapes and sizes, raced back and forth. They stayed in the stream with the yellow line that wasn't made of water.

I stood near Mother, just barely touching her side. We watched for a long time. Listening for more new sounds, I heard only the woodpecker's familiar tapping.

I glanced at Mother. "People really are ugly animals!"

"Those weren't people." Mother smiled. "The small ones are cars. The big ones are trucks. They all have people inside."

I felt my mouth pop open. My eyes got big. "Did the cars eat the people?"

"No." Mother tried not to laugh, but her tummy jiggled. "People made the cars. They get inside them on purpose. People aren't able to run fast like we can. They are always in such a hurry to get someplace else. Then once they get there, they hurry to get back."

"What about the stream that they were on? What is that?"

"Bub Moose, stay away from that! It is a road. The cars and big trucks move along it. They whiz so quickly that a little moose can't get out of their way. Are you listening? This is an important lesson."

"Yes, Mother. I'm listening. It's a road. Stay away!"

Mother smiled. "Come on, we need to move on, Bub Moose. It has been a long day. We need to go into the trees before we settle down for the night."

"Wait, Mother."

"What is it, Bub?"

"See that leaf down beside the road? The great big one that's shaped funny? What kind of tree does that come from? Oh . . . and the one beside it. It looks funny, too, but it's so thin I can see through it."

Mother leaned forward. Her big brown eyes narrowed to tiny slits. Finally she sighed. "Those are not leaves, Bub. The big white one is a piece of paper. I don't know the name for the clear one. It's like paper. The people throw them from their cars. And see over there—that shiny thing?"

"The one that looks like a short tree limb. Like Dudley or one of the other beavers chewed both ends off a branch? It's slick and hard and shiny looking, though."

"That's it." She nodded. "That's a can."

"Is a can a type of tree?"

"No, dear. Paper and cans come from people. They put things inside the papers and the cans. Then when they are through with them, they call them trash. They throw the trash away and clutter up the forest."

"Why are people so messy, Mother?"

She sighed and shook her head. "I don't know, Bub. Some of them are okay. I guess others just don't love the forest. They don't live here, like we do, so they don't take very good care of it." She nudged my rump with her nose. "Let's go find a place to spend the night."

We walked to the edge of the forest. Mother began to sniff the ground. She led me to some trees that were leaned up and piled together. These trees looked weird. They were all the same size and flat instead of round. They had no branches or leaves. She walked around sniffing the thing for a long time.

"What kind of trees are these?" I asked.

"These aren't trees, they are boards. People use them to make buildings."

"Buildings?"

Mother smiled. "Yes, Bub. Buildings are like caves. Only instead of finding them in the mountains, people animals make them. They put their caves together in all different sizes. The big ones are sometimes made of rock. They call them buildings. The smaller ones are called cabins and are often made of wood. This is a cabin where people live. They haven't been in this one for a long time, so the smells are almost gone. Put your nose near the door and sniff."

I stepped up closer. Ears perked, I cautiously put my nose down near the edge of the wood. A few new smells came to me. They weren't very strong, but something was different.

"The people will come back when the weather changes some more," Mother said. "Right now we need to find a place for the night. Tomorrow we will see some people up close."

I followed Mother into the dense thicket. We nestled together in the lush green plants.

Mother brushed me with her big thick tongue. I

closed my eyes. Visions of people floated in my head. Mother said that they were all colors and shapes. They must be small to fit inside the cars and trucks. People were slow, Mother said. People could be dangerous.

I blinked my eyes, then tried to go to sleep. Mother's breathing was steady and close. I felt safe. Slowly my head drooped and fell to rest on my legs.

All at once my eyes flashed wide open. Trembling, I staggered to my feet. My legs shook so hard I could barely stand. I had to run! I had to get away!

"Bub! Bub Moose! Wake up!" Mother's voice was soft and tender.

"Mother! Mother, help me. They are horrible."

"Bub, wake up. You're having a bad dream. Open your eyes."

Mother was lying beside where I stood. The night surrounded us, but we were safe in our bed in the thicket. I took a deep breath and relaxed.

"Are you okay now, baby?" Mother licked my cheek with her big tongue. "Are you awake?"

"Oh, Mother, it was terrible. There were these awful things that looked like bugs. I thought they were people.

"They had enormous red and yellow bodies. Their short fat legs dragged them across the ground. Their mouths would open and shut. Sharp teeth gnashed at my face. Huge orange eyes stared at me.

"The monsters kept getting closer. I tried to run. My legs were moving as fast as they could!"

"It's okay, little Bub Moose. It was just a bad dream. People are ugly animals, I must admit, but they aren't as ugly or frightening as they were in your dream. I could feel your legs moving, but you wouldn't wake up. You're all right now, Bub Moose. Try to relax and go back to sleep."

"They were REAL. I could see them. They were right here!" My body was still shaking.

"Don't think about the people anymore. Think about being back at the pond. Think about Dudley and the other beavers there. Nothing is going to hurt you here."

I tucked myself into a ball. Mother's big body was safe around me. There really wasn't any reason to be afraid. Suddenly I heard a lonely howl from the edge of the forest. I looked up at Mother.

"Wolves, Bub Moose. Remember we heard them at the pond. It's okay. We are safe." Mother lay quietly. Her ears were perked, but she didn't move.

I twitched my ears and listened, too. I heard another solitary call before the forest was quiet again.

The next time I opened my eyes, streams of sunshine filtered through the tall trees. It was finally morning. I could hardly wait to go see the people.

Chapter 5

Opening my eyes, I stayed very still as I looked around for Mother. She was browsing nearby. I perked my ears and listened for danger. No strange or scary sounds came. Feeling safe, I stretched my legs out in front of me, stood up, then shook the night away. I hurried to her side for breakfast.

When I was finished, I was ready to go see the people. Mother wasn't ready. Seemed like I always had to wait for Mother. Pestering her wouldn't help, either, but I did it anyway—not a lot, though. The forest was a good place to explore while I passed the time. Venturing slowly around an open area, I kept my eyes on her. The grass wasn't very thick, but it was soft and sweet. Leaning down, I took a bite. It wasn't bad. Each day, as I grew bigger, I found there were more things I could eat. Nothing was as good as Mother's milk, but she told me I needed to try different foods. I grazed until I saw Mother looking for me. Bouncing to her side, I smiled up at her beautiful face.

"Are you ready, Bub Moose? We will go to the people place now." Mother nudged me and gave me a sweet kiss with her big tongue.

"I'm ready, Mother." I perked my ears to show her that I remembered to listen for sounds of danger.

I was so excited, though, that my tail switched back and forth all by itself.

"You're a good little moose, Bub. Follow me."

Staying close, I brushed Mother's leg as we walked along a trail. The safe sounds of the forest were all around us as the birds chirped their morning calls. I watched and remembered the path as we strolled toward the people place.

At last we came to a huge lake. Mother led me into it for a drink.

"We are very close, Bub Moose. While I browse, I want you to rest. You will be able to see where the people are, but you must not go to the cliff until I am ready to take you. Do you understand?" Mother's big eyes looked straight into mine.

"What's a cliff?" I asked.

"Follow me, little one." Mother led me to the edge of the mountain. "This is a cliff."

My eyes were open as wide as I could get them. In front of me there was nothing. I stretched my neck to see where the hill went, but it wasn't there. Taking another step forward, there was still nothing. I rocked back, making sure most of my weight was over my hind legs. Then very very slowly, one inch at a time, I leaned to look over.

The hill was really steep. There were no trees or grass, just dirt and rock, but it wasn't as bad as I thought. I felt myself relax some as I leaned out a little more.

Up in the high mountain I'd climbed rocks that were steeper than this. One time I climbed up real high while Mother was browsing in the pond.

"This is a cliff, Bub Moose. You must stay back away from it."

"It's not that bad," I said. "It's not as steep as the big rock near Dudley's pond."

Mother's eyes got tight and she flared her big nose at me. "The dirt is loose and dangerous. Stay away from the edge. I want you to lie down and wait. Do you see the buildings?" Mother looked down into the valley.

"I see them . . . I think. The building things are sort of like mountains, only different. But . . . Mother . . . can you go through the building/cabin thing again? Buildings are big, so big people live in them. Cabins are small, so smaller people live in those. Right? I'm not quite sure which is which."

Mother lowered her head and gave me a little wink. "I'm not too sure, either, Bub. It *is* very con-

fusing. When I was not much older than you, I spent a long time watching a people town. The easiest way to remember is that the cabins are usually smaller. The buildings are usually bigger.

"People are pretty much the same size. Since the buildings are larger than the cabins, they have more people inside. The way I figured it out was that they live in the cabins. They get up in the morning and rush to the big buildings. They spend the day there, then rush back to the small cabins to spend the night." She shook her head and sighed. "Strange animals."

"I can see the buildings." I frowned. "And I can see some cabins. But how will I know when I see people?"

"Watch for movement near the buildings. The people will come out of them. You'll see. I will be browsing in the meadow. You will be safe here." Mother gave me a goodbye kiss with her long tongue and strolled toward the pond.

I folded my legs and laid down close to the edge of the cliff—but not too close. I watched Mother until she sloshed into the water, then turned my eyes toward the buildings.

At first I thought they were small mountains. But as I looked at them more closely, I knew that my mother was right. These mountains weren't natural. The sides were all straight up and down and all the same. Mountains were all different.

There was a very big building near the bottom of the cliff. The rocks on it were all red, all the same size, and all stacked one on top of the other. Real rocks were all different shapes and sizes. The top of the biggest building was flat instead of pointy. All along the sides, the square-shaped shiny spots glared back at me. They were bright and glistening like the surface of a pond. But they were stuck on the sides of the buildings. Water couldn't do that. Water had to stay in a pond or stream. I wondered how many people could be inside the building. Were there lots of people inside? How big were the people?

"Ringggg!" A piercing sound came to my ears. For a second I wanted to jump up and run to Mother. Instead I stayed very still, keeping my eyes on the building where the sound had come from. As I watched, small movements tumbled out of an opening. Squealing noises replaced the ringing sound.

The movement was made by some kind of small animals. They raced across the grass behind the building, like ripples racing across a pond. The little animals scampered everywhere. It was a long way down and hard to see, but even this far off, I could tell that people were really weird. Each one was different. Their front legs didn't touch the ground. Their hind legs were as long as mine. That's how they moved, reared up and running on their back legs. Their fur was all different colors—some red like the high mountain sumac, some green like the meadow grass. Others had fur as blue as the beaver pond. A few even had brown fur almost the color of mine. All of them had naked faces. They didn't have a muzzle, and their noses were so tiny I could barely see them. Without hair, I bet their naked faces got really cold when the sun went behind the mountain. I wanted to get closer to see how they could move around with their front legs in the air.

Mother was coming out of the water. I leaped up and ran to her.

"I saw the people! Can we go closer?" I was bouncing against her.

"Not now, Bub Moose. We will get closer, but we need to stay in the safety of the forest. You can watch a little longer."

"Can I go down the cliff, just a little way? I'll be careful."

"No! Stay away from the cliff!" Mother moved off to nibble some of the green shoots of meadow grass.

I bounded to my spot and lay back down near the edge of the cliff. The people below were jumping and running in the space near the building. Two of the people were bigger than the rest. They must have been the mothers. When they made their mouth noises, the smaller people would run to them. One people clunked another people on the head with his hoof. When the big people made a mouth noise at him, he walked real slow to stand in front of her. She put her front hooves on her sides and leaned down to look at him. When she finished, his head hung low and he turned and went inside the building. These animals were really interesting. Weird—but interesting.

"Ringgg!" The little people suddenly ran toward the building. They stood one behind the other near the two bigger ones. Then slowly they started to disappear inside. I strained my eyes. It was like watching a garter snake disappear into a hollow log. There were other movements in the valley—a few tiny cars, a truck, and a few people animals—but nothing as interesting as the little people.

I twitched my ears and closed my eyes. I was a bit sad that they were gone, but maybe they would be back. A short nap would help the time pass quickly. I was almost asleep, when I heard a new sound.

"Sniff, sniff." The sound was getting closer. Keeping my body very still, like Mother taught me, I slowly opened my eyes.

Right in my face was the fuzziest thing I had ever seen. The ball of white fur scooted back when I jerked my head up.

"What *are* you?" I asked.

The thing ran a few steps toward the trees. It stopped suddenly and turned its fleecy face to me. Two blue eyes stared.

"What are *you?*" The thing made bold steps toward me.

When I scrambled to my feet, the white fuzzy thing backed up again.

I stood up as tall as I could. "I **am** Bub Moose! Now what are you?"

The little thing didn't look very big in my shadow, but he puffed up his chest and stepped bravely toward me. "Grrr, I **am** Wolf!"

I remembered Mother telling me that as long as I was little, wolves were dangerous. But I was lots bigger now. This guy didn't look so tough.

"You're a wolf? You don't look very scary to me." I stretched taller and stepped toward him. This time he didn't back up.

"Grrr, I am Wolf and you had better look out for me!" He turned his body to the side and glared.

"I'm not afraid of you. I am lots bigger, and I can kick you off this cliff with one big bump. What's your real name? Dudley helped pick out my name. You must have a real name, too. What is it?" I dropped my head and looked him in the eye.

Wolf's ears flattened against the sides of his furry face. He scratched his neck with his back leg. "I guess that you can call me Snow. My mother says that I look like snow—whatever that is. She says that soon everything will look just like me . . . Snow."

The wolf had white shaggy fur and a long bushy tail. He wasn't beautiful like Mother. His nose was short and pointy with a black spot on the end.

"I've never seen a wolf," I said. "Mother said wolves were big and scary. You're not big at all. In fact, you're a lot smaller than I am. Why do you make all those noises at night?"

"That's not just me. That's my pack—my mother, father, their brothers and sisters, and the little ones." Snow took a short bounce toward me. "Hey, want to play tag?"

"What's tag?" I watched him cautiously.

Suddenly Snow leaped at me and bounced against my leg. "That's tag! Now you have to touch me back."

"I've never done this before," I said.

"Hey, it's fun. My brothers and sisters play it with me all the time. Just touch me." Snow scooted away, then jumped back at me.

Carefully I moved toward him. He darted away, then stopped.

"Bet you can't touch me," he said with a flip of his tail. "Touch me, Bub Moose! Tag me if you can."

"Okay, here I come!" Leaping forward, I suddenly stumbled and fell right on my nose. It hurt, but not very bad. It just made me feel *really* dumb. I scrambled to my feet.

"You missed me, Bub. Try it again. You can do it!" His long white tail jerked one way and then the other.

I leaped up, lowered my head, and charged toward him.

"Missed again, Moose. Mother says to concentrate. Look at what you are going to nip at and then aim. You can't miss."

I looked at that fluffy tail. I thought about how flippy it was. I darted toward it.

"Yippppp!" Snow fell to the ground and licked his tail. "Ouch, that was pretty good."

"Thanks. Did I hurt you?" I watched as he jumped back up and started toward me again.

As I lowered my head, I shifted my weight so I could make a quick escape if I needed to. Snow was looking at my hind leg. I tried to flip my back end away from his stare.

"Grrrr, here I come." Snow dodged one way, then the other as he shot toward my back leg.

Fear suddenly came over me. I glanced toward the pond. I didn't see Mother. I had to take care of myself. My back leg gave a quick jerk at the wolf. My hoof hit him in the side.

"Yip, yip, yap," the wolf howled. When Snow quit tumbling, he started licking his side. "Not so hard, Bub Moose. We're only playing."

"I've never played with anyone but Mother before. I got a little scared. I'm sorry. Are you okay?" I looked at Snow, but I tried to stay alert because I wasn't sure what he was going to do.

Leaping up, Snow jumped toward me again. "You can't hurt a wolf. We're tough."

"That howl didn't sound like you were tough. It

sounded like you were hurt. Should I call my mother over here?"

"No, let's just play. Tag, you're it!" Snow bumped me on the side.

"That's not fair." I pouted.

"Anything is fair in tag. Come get me." Snow's blue eyes stared straight at me.

I charged at him and missed. Stretching my legs, I pretended to flip my ears at a fly. Instantly I darted toward him. "Got you, Snow!"

"That's good, Bub! You get better every time." Snow crouched on the ground with his head low and his ears perked. Blue eyes narrowed as he stared at me.

That's when I saw them. Looming behind Snow were five huge creatures with their teeth bared. A low-pitched growl came from one of the enormous beasts. I backed up a step, just as Snow leaped at me.

Suddenly we were both falling and sliding at the same time. Tumbling, Snow and I scraped and bumped as we fell over the edge of the cliff.

Chapter 6

Get off me, you big lug!"

Snow's voice seemed far away. I shook my head and blinked, trying to remember what happened. My legs felt like they had knots in them. Everything was spinning. One minute I was tumbling—rolling over and over—then I stopped. Only trouble, my head *didn't stop.* It kept going round and round, and my eyes jerked and jumped and bounced.

"Scoot over, I can't move!" Something shoved against my back.

"Huh?" I tried to look around.

"I said, scoot over. I can't move." Snow's little paws pushed again.

I tried to kick my legs free, but they were kind of stuck, some place down under me. Snow pulled and wiggled and twisted and shoved. I kept trying to get my legs to work so I could stand. I really needed to get up, look around, and try to figure out what happened.

"You're smushing my leg," Snow growled.

"I can't help it. It's wrapped around my leg and . . . and this leg, here, is under that leg and . . . and . . . Where's my other leg? Where's your tail. We're stuck!"

I didn't know about Snow, but *I* felt like a total idiot. We moose are really good about getting to our feet. Standing is the first thing we learn, as little-bitty babies. Being all tangled up and unable to move . . . well, it was disgusting.

With a grunt, Snow finally yanked one leg free. I rolled toward him, then away from him. He got another leg out from under us. Once loose, he hopped around in front of me and glared.

"What were you doing? I thought that we were just playing! The next thing I know you shove me off the cliff."

I shook my head again. "I didn't mean to. I don't even know what happened. We were standing there and then . . . Oh, now I remember! There were big snarling animals behind you. They were enormous and had long, sharp teeth and eyes that burned when they looked at me."

"Animals? Animals? What kind of animals? I didn't see anything. You must have dreamed it."

I straightened out one leg, but the other one

wouldn't move. It was still stuck. Frowning, I tried to look. It was pinned under something, only I couldn't see. I wiggled and leaned to one side. There it was—my front leg was stuck under my back leg. How did I get in such a mess?

Rocking from side to side, I finally got my legs untangled. I scrambled to my feet, kind of shook, then looked down to see what the damage was. It wasn't bad. There was dust and dirt all over me. There was a scratch on my right knee, and my left hip felt kind of sore. Other than that . . .

"What kind of animals," Snow repeated.

I glanced down. Snow was kind of dusty and dirty, too. He didn't seem to be hurt, though. His eyes drew to tiny slits as he stared at me.

"Well?"

"Well, what?"

"The animals."

"Oh, the scary ones. Ah . . . let me think."

"Come on," he urged.

Trying to remember, I closed my eyes.

There had been five big animals standing there. They all had long sharp teeth. Teeth that weren't much good for eating grass or pond roots. Teeth that were mean and scary and pointed. When I'd looked at them, their pink lips curled back, and I could see how long and scary those teeth really were.

Just remembering sent a chill through me. Glancing up, I tried to see if they were still there, looking down at us. I couldn't even see where we had been. "Well?"

I peeked down. Snow's head was cocked to one side. His big fluffy tail didn't wag. It just drooped behind him.

With a shrug of my floppy ears, I swallowed. "I don't know what I saw. They looked a little bit like you, only bigger. There were lots of long, sharp, scary teeth and . . . and . . . All I did was step back to get away, and here we are."

Snow gave a little snort and shook himself. Some of the dust and dirt that covered his white fur puffed into the air and drifted away on the wind. Stepping back, I stared up at the mountain. The side was steep and rugged. I sat down on my rear. Snow stood beside me. With me sitting and him standing, we were both about the same size. Eyes wide and mouths opened, we looked up at the cliff.

"You say they kind of looked like me?"

"Yes. Only bigger and they showed me their teeth and they looked at me—real mean."

"Maybe those big animals were my pack. Maybe they saw us playing and thought you were trying to hurt me."

My bottom lip stuck out and kind of wiggled up and down. "I think they wanted to eat me."

Snow leaned over and kissed me with his long pink tongue. "They wouldn't hurt you. You're my friend." He scratched his neck with his back leg. "I bet they thought I needed help. I wouldn't let them hurt you. You would be safe with me."

For a long time we sat, staring at the steep slope. Finally I looked over at my friend. Snow's bottom lip stuck out and quivered up and down like mine. "How are we going to get back up there?" He sniffed. "How are we going to get back home?"

"My mother told me to stay away from the cliff." Now my lip was twitching again. "She said that it was dangerous and that I couldn't get back if I came down here. She is going to be worried if she can't see me!" A knot tightened up in my throat. It felt a lot like the very first time I tried to eat grass instead of Mother's milk. This knot was different, somehow. It made my stomach feel wiggly and made my bottom lip bounce so much that I couldn't control it.

"Hooowl, yip, yip!"

The sound made me jump. I looked. Snow's head was up, his neck stretched out. "Hooowl, yip, yip, yip!"

Snow made it look like a big deal. It was a tiny sound, though, that I could barely hear. Frowning, I studied him for a moment.

"What are you doing?"

"I'm calling for my pack, what do you think?"

"I think you sound silly! They can't hear you with that little yapping sound. We are too far away, and besides, what would they do anyway?" That knot tightened in my throat again, especially when I thought about what they might do—to me.

"They will come get me. As soon as they can, they will come and rescue us." Snow started to howl again.

"Hush, let's see if we can find our own way up." I jumped to my feet and climbed. But the more I tried to climb, the steeper it seemed to get. I didn't go very far. Each time I took a step, the ground moved out from under me. Small pebbles bounced and clattered and rolled. I climbed faster. It only made more of the loose rocks scamper from under my hooves. I stopped. Snow was next to me. Puffing hard for air, he stopped, too. My head hung low.

"Maybe we can find a different place to go up. It might be easier in another spot. There must be a slope that's not so steep. Come on."

Snow followed me along the edge of the mountain. As we walked, I thought about Mother. When she came back to the cliff, she would look for me in the safe nest where she had left me. I wouldn't be there. Mother wouldn't be able to find me if we moved very far. I stopped dead in my tracks.

"We need to stay put," I said. "We need to go back where we were. Mother won't be able to find me if we move."

Snow's pointy nose twitched one way, then the other. "Yeah, but she couldn't see us where we were, either."

I looked up once more. Snow was right. The mountain was too steep. We couldn't even see the top. I sighed and followed my friend. We walked a short distance along a narrow ledge. When that path disappeared, we had to scoot down another little hill. Suddenly Snow's bushy tail shot straight up. Loose rock scattered under his paws and he tumbled. Leaning forward, I peeked over the little ledge where he had vanished. Snow was already on his feet. He shook himself, real hard. Dust flew in all directions. Carefully I climbed down beside him. My big hooves helped me stay steady.

"Hey, Bub, how are you doing?" Snow shook again and wagged his tail as if trying to pretend he hadn't fallen.

"I'm okay, but shouldn't we be going up, instead of down?"

"Nah! We have to find the right spot. We may have to go down before we can find the perfect place to go back up." We stood together looking at the mountain.

"Are you sure?"

"Sure, I'm sure. My pack has been all over this mountain. There has to be a place to get back up. We just have to find it."

That knot was back in my throat and tummy. "This is my first time away from our pond. I want to go home. I want my mother."

"Trust me. We have been everywhere on this

mountain. There has to be a way back up. Just be patient."

I raised my head and puffed out my chest big and proud. I wasn't scared anymore. Snow knew the way back.

"You've been here." I smiled. "You've been this close to the people?"

"Well, no. Not exactly *here.*" Snow glanced back over his shoulder at me. "Mother says that people are the most dangerous animals in the forest. She never let me come down here before."

"But . . . but, you said you'd been all over the mountain. You said . . ."

Snow gave a little snort. "I have been all over the mountain. But the mountain is up there." He pointed with his little black button nose. "This is the valley. I haven't been here before, but if we can find the right place . . . I just know . . ."

My head drooped and the air whooshed out of my proud chest. I didn't feel so brave anymore. I wanted my mother!

I tried to remember all the lessons she had taught me. I couldn't think of anything that would help. I listened for the safe sounds of the meadow. They weren't there. My ears flopped one way, then the other. I couldn't hear woodpecker's familiar *tap, tap, tap.* All I could hear were the pads of Snow's paws crunching on the loose rock.

I followed him as he zigzagged farther down the

mountain. Keeping my eye on Snow, just like I did when I followed Mother, we made our way clear to the bottom. There I stopped. Sighing, I looked longingly up the steep hill with the loose rocks. Mother would find me. . . . Mother just *had to* find me!

"*Ringgg!*"

My heart stopped. My eyes flashed wide.

"*Ringgg!*" The loud, horrible sound came again.

Snow and I froze in our tracks. We looked up. The mountain—I mean building—where the people had been was right in front of us. Suddenly it burst open. Through the opening, it looked like a cave Mother had shown me in the mountains. Little people rushed from the cave, screaming and giggling and making all sorts of strange noises.

Eyes wide, all I could do was watch as they poured out. Snow crouched down, but like me, all he could do was stand there.

"Hey, look at the moose," a voice came to my ears. The noises got louder and louder as the small animals moved toward us.

"Yeah," another voice squealed. "There's a dog with him, too."

"That's not a dog!" yet another voice chimed in. "That's a wolf!"

Heart pounding inside my chest, I tried to back up. Loose rocks slid beneath my hooves.

At the very same instant Snow and I turned around. We raced for the slope and climbed. We had to get away from these dangerous creatures. We ran as hard and fast as we could. Rocks scraped and scattered and tumbled. We ran harder. More rocks slipped away. We ran as hard as we could.

Only trouble . . . no matter how hard we ran . . . we didn't go any place.

Finally—exhausted and gasping for breath—we fell.

The little people were all around us. I tried to jump to my feet, but I was so tired. Snow wiggled beneath me. My nostrils flared. My eyes sprang wide. My ears perked.

The people were everywhere. They came closer and closer and . . .

We were goners. Mother was right, people were dangerous, and they were going to get us.

I closed my eyes and waited for the end.

Chapter 7

Wide-eyed I watched the people move closer. All at once a big person stepped in front of the others. She raised her front hoof. She held a little silver thing in it. It was as sparkly as a dew drop, but larger. She held the silvery dew drop to her lips and took a deep breath. A loud shrill *tweet* came from her mouth. I guess she was like Mother. The little ones knew her special *hronk* or *tweet*. Instantly the small people looked at her and got very quiet. They backed away just a bit. My legs were so wobbly I could barely stand. My knees were scratched and sore. Everything inside told me to run, but I was too weak. I just couldn't do it.

The big person's front legs reached out. She inched, ever so slowly, toward me. Something about her look—her tender smile—quieted the scared feeling inside of me.

Her small blue eyes were soft. Her back legs took short steps toward me. Looking again at her face, I felt that she was friendly. I don't know why, but her lips were stretched upward. The little people were making quiet noises, but they didn't move any closer. I tried to think of Mother's lessons. The only one that I could remember was *Stay away from people.*

Except this people didn't look dangerous. The two front feet were in the air, but she wasn't pawing or trying to hit me. Just short legs reaching out slow and gentle.

A warm feeling went over me as something touched my head, then rubbed my neck.

"Grrrrrr . . . Get away from my friend!" Snow threatened from behind me.

I glanced back at him. "Why are you making that racket?"

"The people are hurting you," Snow growled. "I'm warning them to stay away."

"It really doesn't hurt," I told him. "In fact, this feels pretty good. How can it hurt me?" The person gently scratched behind my ears and neck. "I like this. It feels friendly, not scary at all. Be quiet, they aren't even near you."

When I looked back, two small people were coming close to my face. I twitched my ears.

Small hooves reached out and rubbed my cheek and chin. It was very nice to have gentle rubs. I thought about Mother's sweet kisses. A feeling of sadness swept over me when I remembered that she wasn't anywhere near. I couldn't get away from the small people, so I just stood there. A few of the little ones came closer, then they stepped back, and some more filed up to touch me. Nobody tried to get close to Snow. He hid behind me, crouching low. Occasionally I could hear a soft "Grrrr . . ."

My legs were getting wobbly.

"*Ringggg.*"

Reluctantly, almost one at a time, the people turned away and moved back toward the building.

Exhausted, I plopped down on my rump. My eyes closed and the rest of my body fell into a heap. Still watching the people, Snow eased around to my face and sniffed me.

"See, I told you they would hurt you." Snow shoved at my legs with his snout.

"I'm not hurt. I'm just sooooo tired. The people felt good against my body. It was kind of like Mother. I just need a quick nap." My eyes felt heavy as I drifted off. I thought about Mother's beautiful face looking down at me.

I don't know how long I slept, but when I opened my eyes again, long shadows stretched across the grass. Snow was tucked up against me, asleep. When I straightened my legs, I shoved him away a little.

Snow's eyes flashed. He jumped up, looking around for danger.

"Geerrrrr!" He tried to sound mean and tough. When he didn't see any of the people close, he blinked. "What's going on?"

"I just need to move a little." I stretched my legs out as far as I could. Hopping up, hind end first, I felt much stronger now.

Snow gave a shake. "Are you ready to move on? Our pack doesn't stay anywhere very long, and we have been here quite a while."

I glanced toward the building. "Are those people still in there?"

Snow shrugged his ears. "I fell asleep, but I usually hear noises. I haven't heard any more of the sounds that bring them outside. Let's get going. It'll be dark soon. My pack will be looking for me."

Keeping our distance, we watched the building for any movement. We walked a little ways from the place where we had come down. I felt stronger after my rest, so we tried again. The climb was still much too steep. Snow clawed at the rocks and pebbles but for every step he went up, he slid back two.

"We've got to go down some more. This isn't a good spot to get up the mountain." Snow pranced off ahead of me.

I hesitated. "There are too many buildings and people down there. Somebody is going to hurt us."

Snow tilted his head to the side. "So what are you going to do? Just sit here? Those little people will be back. We have to find a better place to climb up." Snow rubbed his face against my neck.

"Hronk!" I squeaked.

Snow jumped away from me. "What was *that!*"

"That was me. I am calling for Mother. She will know what to do when she finds me." I raised my chin to call once more.

"Wait. Stop! The people will come out here. You don't want them to hurt you again, do you?"

"Nobody hurt me that first time. They were gentle and kind. Maybe they will find my mother and bring her to me." I ducked my head to look Snow in the eye. He leaned his head to the side.

"I don't think so. If they did find your mother they wouldn't know how to tell her where her baby was. We have to do this on our own. Let's go, NOW!" Again Snow trotted off down the path that led toward more people buildings.

I thought about what he said. It made sense. Mother didn't like the people, either. She wouldn't know what they were trying to tell her. Snow was right. We had to go on our own. Cautiously I followed my furry friend. I kept my eyes on his fluffy tail. The big buildings loomed tall and close so I tried to think of the beautiful meadow where I belonged—where I felt safe.

We found a path where the ground was hard and black. It looked like a car road, but I wasn't sure. There were no stripes down the middle. The mountain, where we came from, was on one side of us and the buildings were on the other. Stopping in front of me, Snow sniffed the air. A strange odor came to my nostrils. Stretching his neck, Snow searched for the smell. His little black nose jiggled back and forth.

"What is it?" I asked, watching him.

"It's food. I'm hungry!"

"What kind of food?" I frowned. "I eat tender morsels of grass, but mostly, I get milk from Mother. What food smells like that?"

The little black button on the tip of Snow's snout leaned toward the smell. His tail wagged. "I don't know. But it smells wonderful!"

"We don't have time. Our mothers are waiting for us to come back to them. We'll get plenty of food then." I started walking along the road. Snow followed me, but his nose kept wiggling in the air.

"Here's that smell! It's coming from the trash can." Snow stopped and pointed with his nose.

"What's a trash can?" I asked, tilting my head to one side.

"That gray thing over there," Snow answered. "I've got to get some of that delicious food."

"We have to move on," I argued. "You said that you could get us out of here. We don't have time to look around. Come on!"

It was too late, Snow had already headed toward the back of the building.

"It won't take long. I eat fast. Come on, you can watch out for the people. They seem to like you."

The little wolf trotted straight to a shiny, round gray thing that was taller than he was. He started jumping at it, shoving and hitting it with his paws. With a little *clank* it finally tipped over and the top fell off. Snow started digging at the stuff that tumbled out.

"Come on, Bub, this is good food. My pack eats it sometimes. But just the *fresh* meat—not the yucky stuff." He licked his lips, rooting and searching through the mess.

"I don't eat that! We need to go." I couldn't believe it. The wolf tore and jerked, searching through the pile of junk that had poured out from the gray thing. He gobbled as much of the meat as he could find.

A noise made my ears stand straight up. Looking around, I saw a glistening square on the side of the building. It was clear as water in a mountain stream—only it didn't flow. It just sat there. One of the people looked through from the other side. He smiled at me. I could hear strange sounds from inside the building, but the people didn't come out.

Snow must have heard the noises, too. He jumped away from the pile on the ground.

"Let's get out of here!" he yelped. Tail between his legs, he loped off. "Those people will get us!"

"They were inside the building. They're not going to get us." I sighed and turned to follow Snow.

I had to hurry to keep up with my friend as he trotted away.

"Grrr . . . Yap . . . yap . . . yap!"

The loud sound made my legs lock. Snow backed up until his tail crunched against my knee. Beside us was a row of white boards. The sound came from behind them. I leaned my head down, staring. Through the gaps between the wood, I saw three big animals. They looked a lot like Snow.

"Is it your pack?" I asked. "They look kind of like you. They even sound like the wolves in the meadow."

Snow was behind me, trembling. "No, these guys aren't my pack! They are mean and ugly. They want to get us."

"Grrrr. Yap . . . yap . . . yap!" They barked and snarled. They leaped and slammed against the boards, but I guess they couldn't get out.

"They don't look too dangerous to me," I said.

"Can't you hear what they are saying?"

"Grrr. Yap . . . yap . . . yap?" I asked.

"No! They want to tear us up. They said that they were dogs and they rule the town. We are in their territory and we have to get out—now! If we don't get away from their fence, they are going to eat us up."

"No, I didn't hear that. They just yapped. But that's okay, we need to go anyway." I quickened my pace and cantered off. Snow stayed right on my heels. He looked scared or worried, because his head hung low on one end and his tail drooped low on the other.

More yapping followed us as we moved on our way. People came out of their buildings—I guess they were cabins, because they were small—to stare at us. Snow crouched even lower and crept along behind me. Nobody got close to us like the little people did. They just stood still and watched as we jogged past. After we got away from the yapping dogs, Snow straightened up.

"How are you doing, Bub? You weren't scared, were you?" He took a deep breath and puffed out his chest. "Dogs talk pretty ough, but we could have taken them."

I blinked and stared down at him. "What are you talking about, Snow? You said those big animals were going to eat us. You were afraid of them."

"Nah. We could have beaten them." Snow's tail flipped in the air. "Your big hooves would have saved us. I could have sneaked around and jumped all over them." Snow looked back at me. "We could have done it."

"GRRRR. We'll see who's tough!" A huge shaggy brown dog stood right in front of us. There was no row of white boards—no fence. He was just there! On the road—staring us in the eye!

Chapter 8

Yip, yip! Run, Bub, run!" Snow barked.

My hooves clomped on the black road as I chased after my friend. I could hear his yipping in front of me. We raced away from the cabins to escape the horrible beast. In my mind's eye I could see him chasing right behind us. I could almost feel his sharp white fangs snapping inches from my legs.

I ran harder. My heart pounded in my chest.

At the edge of the forest I spotted Snow trying to hide behind a clump of trees. I glanced back over my shoulder. The scary beast with the sharp fangs was no longer in sight. I was wheezing and puffing when I caught up with him. Snow's eyes were as wide as could be.

"Was *that* thing part of your pack?" I looked down at the panting wolf.

"That was another DOG! That was a mean dog! A *really* mean dog! He was running free, and he may be right behind us." Snow shook his fur. "My daddy would tear him up if he was here."

"He didn't even follow us. He's probably still standing there yapping at the air. Do you have any idea how we're going to get back to the mountaintop? My mother must be very worried about me."

"My pack will find us. We just have to keep watching for them." Snow didn't seem quite as sure of himself as before. He plopped on his rump in the grass and scratched his ear with a hind foot.

I sighed. My head hung low. "I'm hungry. I need my mother."

The shadows from the trees seemed to race across the ground. They grew longer with each passing moment. Soon the sun would go hide behind the mountains. It would be dark and lonely and scary. We had to find our way home. I started walking again. Still panting, Snow followed me from the trees and into a small meadow.

Suddenly I saw her. Mother was standing near the center of the clearing. She nibbled on a pile of dry-looking grass.

"Mother!" Eyes wide and heart pounding, I bounded toward her. The closer I got, the more excited I was! "Mother, it's me!"

The big animal turned around and glared at me. "Mooo! I don't know you."

I didn't even look at her. Mother never said "Moo" to me before, but I was so excited and *so hungry*, I didn't even listen.

"Mother, it's me, Bub!" I raced to her and leaned down to get some warm milk.

A huge hoof flew out. It almost clunked me on the nose.

"Mooo! Get back. I'm not your mother."

I stepped away and blinked. The animal was big, like Mother. She had brown eyes, like Mother. But her face was not long and beautiful. She had sharp pointed things on her head near her short ears. She stomped her hooves at me.

"I'm sorry." My head hung low, and I couldn't look her in the eye. "We're lost. When I first saw you . . . well . . . I miss my mother so so much . . . I . . . I wanted you to be her. I know you are not my mother. I just . . . just . . ."

The big brown animal glared at me. Then her look softened.

"I understand. When I was a little calf, the farmer took me away from my mother. I missed her so much and I was so hungry, I chased a horse all over the pasture." She blinked and wobbled her head at me. "I'm Daisy. I'm a dairy cow. This meadow is my home. I'm not your mother, but you may share my hay. My milk is for the family that takes care of me, though. Maybe if you stay here, your mother will find you. Does she live nearby?"

"I don't know. We were on the mountain and we fell off. We have been looking all day. We are trying to get back up, but we can't find the right place." Suddenly I felt very tired and hungry.

The shadows of the forest were longer. It was almost dark. Snow crouched in the tall grass near the trees.

"Wheeee . . . tweet . . . tweet!" A human sound came to my ears. It was sharp and loud. When I looked toward the sound, I saw a big building. A people stood near it.

"I've got to go. The family needs me at the barn." The cow turned and waddled toward the building.

Sticking my nose into the pile of hay on the ground, I munched on it for a while. It wasn't very good, but I ate some anyway. I felt nervous. I wished that I could feel brave. The wind blew harder as darkness swallowed us. Snow moved closer. We were alone, apart from the rest of the world. I had to be fearless, I couldn't let Snow feel how scared I really was. I had never been away from Mother at night. Inside, my stomach was churning from hunger and fear.

I settled down into the hay. Snow nestled against my back watching the other direction. We would figure out what to do in the morning. We were both worn out and needed some sleep.

The morning light streamed into the pasture. Snow lay on his back with his front legs folded by his chest. His hind legs stuck straight out. My tummy churned and growled. Another sound came to my keen ears. I looked up.

Two people stared down at us. They were really close.

Startled, I jumped and clamored to my feet. Snow sprang up, too.

"Yip," he said, scampering off to the edge of the meadow. "People! Again!"

I started to run, but I didn't. There was something about the little people's eyes that held me where I was. Something caring. Something gentle.

The smaller people held out its front legs. I saw her hooves. They weren't like mine. My hooves only had one cleft or split down the middle. They were strong and sturdy and hard. Her hooves had a whole bunch of splits. Instead of hard and black, they were soft. They were wrapped around something—holding it.

Clear and shimmering like water, what she held wasn't water. It didn't move. Maybe it was ice. Mother had told me about ice. She said it was clear like water, only hard. I tilted my head to the side. There was something white and creamy looking inside the ice. My nose twitched. Whatever it was, it smelled delicious. Moving closer, my lips wiggled as I reached out to touch the warm soft thing at the tip of the ice.

It was food!

I licked my lips. It was like Mother's milk. I couldn't stop as I pulled at the warm yummy liquid that came from inside.

"See, he's just hungry." The big people spoke very soft and gentle. "Hold the baby bottle steady and don't make any fast moves. The moose is easy. Let's see if we can get this little wolf to eat the dog food."

The big person stepped away and dropped to one knee. I stopped sucking the warm milk and looked around. Snow was still crouched at the edge of the meadow near the trees. I shook my head and grabbed at the milk again.

The big person dumped something out on the ground, stood up, and stepped back. My person watched me closely. I looked up into the face. Her small strange-looking hoof reached out slowly and touched my nose. I wasn't the least bit afraid, now. These people made me feel comfortable.

The big person held her hooves up to her face. She had a black box or rock or something. Suddenly a bright light flashed. It made me blink. For a second all I could see was a blue dot.

"Thanks, Mom. The kids at school would never believe it without a picture. I don't believe it myself. He is so cute and cuddly. Do you think he will find his way home? What about the wolf? How do you think the two of them ended up together?"

"I really don't know. They're an odd pair. We have

to go, Leah. If we handle them too much, their mothers might reject them. The little moose has had enough milk to get his strength back. The wolf will get the scent of the dog food when we leave." The little one pulled the last of the warm milk from my lips and stepped back. Then they walked away.

The moment they were gone, Snow raced toward me. Sliding to a stop at the pile on the ground, he sniffed and sniffed. Then he started gobbling it up.

"I was starving." Wagging his tail, Snow paused and gave a little burp. "That was pretty good stuff. Not as good as a juicy MOUSE, but it'll do for now. We better get out of here before they come back and hurt us."

I cocked my head to the side. "Did anybody hurt you? You keep saying that, and nobody has hurt us yet. I like the people. Their touch feels good, and those people brought us some yummy food."

Snow's sharp pointed ears twitched.

"We've just been lucky."

Both of my ears pointed at my friend. "Do you really know where we are going?"

Snow puffed his chest out. Then his shoulders sagged.

Tall trees, short trees, they all seemed the same as we moved along the dirt trail. We found a road. It still wasn't like the one Mother showed me. It didn't have lines down the middle. We followed it anyway. There were cabins on either side of the road. Sort of like the trees, they all began to look the same after a while. Snow trotted on in front of me. My legs felt heavy, but my big hooves kept moving.

Noises came from somewhere ahead of us. There were strange sounds and unusual smells. The clamor grew louder as we moved along. It made both of us nervous. Our pace slowed until we stopped, held our breath, and listened.

Snow glanced over his shoulder at me. His whiskers wiggled up and down on either side of his snout.

"I know that noise." He blinked, but he kept looking at me. "I've heard it before. Mother has a name for it. If I could only remember. . . ."

A steady *thump, thump, thump* came. Relaxed and low, like the beat of my heart, it almost made the rest of the racket seem connected or together, somehow.

"Music!" Snow yipped. "That's what it is— music."

My nostrils flared and crinkled up. "What's that?"

"The sound. That's what Mother calls it. The sound is called music. I heard it one evening when we sat in the woods and watched some campers."

"Campers?"

"Yeah." Snow nodded. "That's people who come and stay in the woods in tents."

"Tents? What are tents?"

Snow gave me a disgusted look. "Tents are like
the cabin caves that people live in. Only these cabins have soft walls that flop in the breeze. People
can fold them up and carry their cabins around on
their backs."

"No way!"

"Yeah. Really." Snow nodded. "I've seen them.
Honest."

I looked up the road where we stood. There were
cars on either side. They didn't whiz or race past, so
I guess they were asleep. All they did was sit. Still,
there were a whole lot of them. The noise—or
music, as Snow called it—came from someplace
beyond where all the cars were.

It wasn't bad, but with all the cars around and all
the cabins on our left and the buildings on our
right . . . I just knew there had to be people.

"I don't like it," I snorted. "The 'music' is getting
too loud. Let's leave."

Off to our right was another road. It was more narrow and darker than the one where we stood. It
went between some tall buildings that were made of
stone. The road was littered with paper and cans and
lots of other . . . other . . . What was that word that
Mother taught me? Oh, yeah. Trash.

"The racket doesn't seem quite so loud, that
way." I pointed with my ears. "Let's go there."

Snow followed me. We moved into the shadows
between the buildings. Cautious and careful, we

eased down the narrow, cluttered road. Beside us
was a big square thing with trash on the ground, all
around it. As tall as I was, it was three times as big
as Snow and me put together. Kind of brown like
the trees, it was hard and cold. Farther down the
road was another and another. I leaned closer to the
one beside us and sniffed.

Suddenly my eyes crossed and my tongue stuck
out the side of my mouth. The smell that came
from the brown box was horrible. For a second I
thought I was going to throw up.

"That's the most disgusting thing I ever smelled
in my life." I gasped, taking a step or two back.

Snow raised up and put his paws on the side of the
big box. He sniffed, only he didn't stagger backward
like I did.

"Garbage."

"Garbage?"

Snow shot me another irritated look. "You sure
don't know much, do you, Bub? Garbage is people
stuff they don't want anymore. They put it in a
place called the Dump. Our cousins, the coyotes,
hang out there all the time. They find all sorts of
rotten meat and chicken scraps. I guess they like the
taste. Us wolves, on the other hand—we like our
meat fresh. No self-respecting wolf would ever eat
out of the Dump. We eat fresh stuff from garbage
cans, at a campsite, of course. I mean the Dump . . .
that's just not cool. It's not something . . ."

"Beep . . . beep . . . beep . . . beep!"

The strange sound stopped Snow right in the middle of what he was saying. Eyes wide, we both spun to see what was making the weird racket behind us. An enormous car came down the path. I guess it was a truck, because it was so big. It had those black hooves that spun round and round. It looked hard and cold, like a truck. Only this thing was huge.

"Beep . . . beep . . . beep . . . beep!" it called over and over as it rolled down the narrow road toward us.

Snow and I scampered to get out of its way. We wanted to run and keep running, but all at once it quit yelling *"Beep, beep!"* at us. Looking back, we saw it stop beside the big brown box that held the stuff my friend called garbage. The thing growled. It stuck out two legs, grabbed the box with the garbage stuff, and lifted it clear off the ground. (The truck must have been really strong, because that box was full of gunk and bigger than Snow and me and even Mother—all put together.)

It growled again. This time it opened its mouth. Right at the very top, this gaping, black, bottomless hole appeared. With his two legs, the truck lifted the garbage box. Holding it above his mouth, he tipped it until all the junk inside poured out. It went right down his throat. Finally the truck monster growled and closed his mouth. Then he put the empty box back on the ground.

Eyes and mouths wide as could be, my friend and I could only watch.

"*Beep . . . beep . . . beep . . . beep,*" it said again. Then it started moving. It came toward us.

"Run, Snow!" I snorted. "Run! It's going to eat us, just like it did that garbage. Run! Run for your life!"

Chapter 9

The Beep-beep Monster quit chasing us. I whipped around and watched the strange beast. He stopped beeping, but . . .

He growled at us!

He growled when he reached out his legs to pick up the next big box. He growled when he opened his enormous mouth. He growled when he swallowed the garbage. Then . . .

"*Beep . . . beep . . . beep . . . beep,*" he said as he started after Snow and me once more.

The white hair raised up on a ridge down Snow's back. "We're not garbage," he snarled. "Quit chasing us!"

"This guy's serious," I warned my friend. "He's really hungry. We'd better get out of here."

Ahead, the walls of the buildings were tall and

steep. There was no space to hide or turn around. No way to slip past and go back the way we had come. Farther down the long, dim, narrow path, I could see light. There was even a green tree.

"This way, Snow. Hurry!"

My friend followed for a ways, then managed to pass me. All of a sudden he stopped. I stopped, too. Only my hard hooves skidded on the black path. I slid right into the back of him. Legs stretched out in front, trying to stop myself, my hooves went under his rump. We sort of crunched together—Snow slid up my legs, and I slid under his hind cnd. Snow stepped from one front paw to the other to keep from falling on his chin. He went up my legs so far that his furry tail flopped me in the nose as it waved back and forth.

"Hey, watch it," he snarled over his shoulder.

"You watch it." I blew at his tail because it was tickling my nose. "You were the one who stopped so quick. What's the deal?"

With a nod of his head, he motioned. There were people at the end of the road. They stood between us and the green safety of the trees. Their backs were toward us. The Beep-beep Monster stopped and got some more to eat. The hungry creature behind us . . . the people in front of us . . . What could we do?

The people didn't seem to see Snow and me . . . not yet. We couldn't get past the monster. There wasn't enough room. We couldn't get too close to the people. Both our mothers had ordered us to stay away from them. And . . . and we couldn't stay here because . . .

"Beep . . . beep . . . beep . . . beep," the beast said, starting after us once more.

"Maybe we should warn the people," I suggested. "They don't even know the monster is sneaking up on them. He could grab them, like he does the boxes, and swallow them in one gulp."

Snow looked at the monster. He looked at the people. He looked back at the monster.

"Let's make a break for it. There aren't very many. Maybe we can dodge between them, slip through, and make it to the trees. Once there, we can find a place to hide."

Sounded like a good idea. There were only two more boxes full of garbage. Hungry as this guy was, he probably wouldn't be satisfied with just two more. That made us next on the menu. I nudged Snow's tail with my nose.

"Let's go!"

Snow slid from his perch on my legs and we charged for the trees. The people yelled when we darted between them. They scattered and hopped out of the way. They pointed and shrieked.

"Look out for the Beep-beep Monster," I warned them with a snort. "He's going to get you."

I guess they didn't understand. They just kept

pointing at Snow and me and making noises with their mouths and laughing. A fat man with no fur on his head accidentally stepped on Snow's front paw.

"Yowwwie!" Snow yelped.

The little fat man lifted his foot and hopped aside. I lowered my head at him. "Watch it, tubby," I warned. "Don't you go stepping on my feet. I'll butt you right in the . . . in the . . ."

Well . . . I didn't have any idea where I was going to butt him. I didn't need to worry about it, either. He saw me coming at him with my head down. He almost knocked two people out of the way when he ran. Once through that crowd, Snow and I found ourselves in the center of a broad road with more people in front of us. This was a *real* road. It was wide, had a stripe down the middle, and it was not crowded or shadowed by the tall buildings. My eyes flashed when I remembered how fast the cars and truck whizzed on the one in the mountains. Mother said roads were dangerous. But nothing seemed to be moving.

"Which way now?" Snow asked.

People lined the edge of the road in front of us. I glanced over my shoulder. More people lined the edge of the road behind us.

"I . . . I don't know where to go."

Suddenly a people voice boomed above all the other noises. It was so loud, it seemed to come from all around—in front of us—behind us—everywhere.

"Ladies and gentlemen, here come our high school football team stars. They made it to the state play-offs last year."

"The tractor and trailer they are riding on was provided by Crutcher's Farm Implement Company," another voice boomed through the air. "The homecoming queen candidates are riding in convertibles from McMahan Buick."

"Let's all put our hands together for the fight song, played by our own Pride of Hidden Valley Marching Band," the first voice said, "and for the future state championship football team."

Snow and I froze in our tracks. We both looked to our right. People—all in rows—were walking away from us. They were really weird looking. All had purple fur with a yellow stripe down the legs. Their heads were purple and hard-looking. A bird roosted on the front of each person's head. One of the people at the rear of the line turned back to look at us. I blinked, realizing it wasn't a bird on his head at all. It was just one big, bright yellow feather.

Down at their sides, the people carried strange things. Some were shiny yellow like the sunset. Others were black and narrow like a tree limb. Still others were the silver of white water on a rushing stream. All at once they lifted the things toward their faces. Strange sounds came. A blast of noise filled the air. It was so loud that it made my ears flatten against my neck. I guess Snow noticed the

startled look on my face, and the way my ears hid from the honks and squeaks and racket. With a blink, he looked up at me and wagged his tail.

"Music."

If this was music, it sounded a lot better when we were farther away.

Right in the middle of the lines of people, a whole row carried tree trunks that were cut off flat on both ends. It wasn't much of a tree trunk, though. The thing was only about as long as it was round. They beat on the tree trunks with sticks and made a pounding noise. One people carried a really big tree trunk. When he hit it with his stick, it made a loud *"BOOM."* Like thunder, I could feel it rattling in my chest.

I didn't want to mess with the people who had purple fur and a feather sticking out of their heads. I guess Snow didn't, either. Slowly he started toward the far side of the road—where we had seen the trees.

Now there were bunches of people there. Our escape to the trees was blocked. Big people and little people were all crowded together.

A tall skinny people, with a fuzzy face, stood in a cabin. The sides flopped with the breeze. That must be what Snow called a tent. "Get your balloons, right here!" he called. "Balloons! Twenty-five cents!"

Little round things that looked like clouds floated

above his tent. Some of the little people had small vines tied to their front legs. The little clouds floated above their heads. They were all different colors and bright as a rainbow. More and more people came to point at us. I could hear voices—not as loud as the two voices that boomed above all the others—but there were so many and the sounds came so close together and the music was so loud . . . I couldn't understand any of it. I looked over my shoulder. The place we came from was crowded now. More people rushed in to clump together. It was like a solid mountain of people.

The people with purple fur and a yellow feather on their heads stopped making the music with their mouths. They turned around to look at us. There was a line of people in front of us, people and the Beep-beep Monster behind us. Snow and I spun to our left and started to run.

The breath froze in my throat. My heart quit beating. My eyes got so big around, I thought they might pop clear out of my head. I slid to a stop and didn't even blink.

Another huge monster rolled toward us. Big and green as the grass, he snarled and growled. Black smoke belched from his head. He had to be a truck, since he was so big and because we were on a road. But he wasn't like any truck I had ever seen before. The two hooves in front were small and close together. His two hind hooves were far apart and bigger than anything I ever saw in my life. They were gigantic. Enormous!

A people car followed close behind him. Only this car was flat, and instead of riding in it, people stood on the thing. These people were covered with purple fur on the top and white fur on the bottom. They didn't have yellow stripes down their legs. Their heads were not covered with fur, like most of the people who lined either side of the road. These people's heads were round and shiny gold. They looked like they were hard as a rock. Little bars hid their faces.

I guess they had been crawling under low branches or something, because some of the purple fur had been scraped off their hides. Each had a different mark where their scratches were: **4 21 18 44.** I bet it hurt to get that much of their purple fur scratched off.

The green monster belched more smoke out of his head. He rolled closer and closer and . . .

Snow spun and tried to run away. His feet slipped on the hard road. With a *whoompf* sound, he fell on his side. Struggling to get up, he was in such a panic and the road was so hard . . . he couldn't get his paws under him. His feet spun and tried to catch the ground. He jerked and flopped, but he couldn't go anywhere.

This was it. This was the end for my friend and me.

"Looks like we have a surprise addition to our homecoming football parade." A voice rumbled and boomed above the clamor of all the rest.

"Maybe they came down from the mountains to wish our team good luck," the second voice said. It was a different voice. Not as deep or rumbly, but it was every bit as loud as the first. "And I think you're right about them wishing our players good luck. They came right up to the John Deere tractor, furnished by Crutcher's Farm Implement Company, and are standing there looking at our football team."

"For those of you up toward Main Street, who can't see down by Johnston's Hardware Store," the deep, rumbly voice said, "we have a baby moose and a little wolf who just came out of the alley. They're a cute pair, but it's kind of weird to see a moose and a wolf together. Wouldn't you say, Kathy?"

"Yes, Bob. Very unusual," the lighter voice answered. "They look a little nervous, too. Now, you folks down on that end of the parade, don't crowd the little things. We don't want to scare them to death."

"Kathy's right. Everybody back up a little. Give them some room. They're really scared and . . ."

I wanted to run. I had to get away.

The green monster blew more smoke from the top of his head. He roared and rumbled. Then—with his round, front hooves just inches from where my friend was struggling to get up off the ground—he stopped. He stayed there, growling and snorting and breathing smoke.

If he took one more step, Snow was a goner. Snow would be smushed flatter than a beaver's tail.

Eyes tight, I lowered my head.

"Back off!" I threatened with a snort. "Get away from my friend!"

The gigantic green beast just snorted back at me. I shook my head and threatened again. He blew black smoke and rumbled.

There was no bluffing this guy like I did the little fat man with no fur on his head. This guy didn't scare.

I wanted to run. If I did, Snow would be left all alone. So frightened that I almost felt sick inside, I knew I couldn't help. I was too little. The green beast was too big. I had to get away!

I turned.

Behind me, I heard Snow's claws scraping on the hard road. I heard him whimper. The enormous green brute roared again.

Scared as I was . . . I just couldn't stand it.

With a snort, I spun back toward the big green monster. I lowered my head. He snorted back at me.

I charged anyway.

I leaped over Snow and butted the ugly beast with my head. I hit him, right in the nose—as hard as I could.

Chapter 1 0

Ouch!

Headache.

Big-time headache!

Something warm and soft and damp touched my nose. I blinked and tried to see what it was. My long lashes fluttered. Snow was standing above me. Head tilted to one side, he watched me with worried eyes. His wet pink tongue flopped out and licked my nose.

"Are you okay?"

I didn't answer. I was a little confused. The last thing I remembered . . . Snow was on the ground, trying to get up. The green monster was snorting and getting ready to eat him and . . . *I* was standing.

Now . . . Snow was standing and I was lying on

my side with a headache that throbbed and pounded so bad, I could hardly keep my eyes open.

"Bub?" Snow repeated. "Are you okay? Are you awake?"

"Yes. Yes, I'm okay," I managed finally. "I'm good."

"That was really brave." Snow kissed my nose again. "Kind of dumb," he added under his breath, "but *really* brave."

I shook my head. The instant I did, I wished I hadn't. It made the pounding come back inside my skull. My eyes blinked and twitched when I stared up at Snow.

"What do you mean, 'Kind of dumb'?"

"Running into a tractor with your head." He motioned with a jerk.

The huge green beast was still on its feet. Quickly I struggled to get my legs under me. My head throbbed, and the whole world spun around. I decided not to get up . . . not quite yet.

"What's a tractor?"

"The thing you ran into. It's a machine—like a people car—only it's bigger and lots heavier."

My eyes crossed when I tried to look up at my head. "It's a lot harder, too."

Snow shrugged his ears. "I guess."

I blinked and shifted my weight. Finally I managed to get on my feet. I was still wobbly, so I tried to focus on Snow.

"What did you say it was?"

"A tractor. I saw one up close once. There's a big pasture down below the waterfalls where we spent the summer. Mama told me what it was. One night my brothers and sisters and I even sneaked up and smelled it."

"I don't care what his name is," I told Snow. "All I know is that he's a lot tougher than I am."

My head wasn't banging so bad, and the world had stopped spinning. Suddenly I noticed the movement around us. People were inching closer. My heart thumped inside my chest. My breathing was hard and loud in my ears. Snow noticed the people crowding in on us, too. I saw him tremble. Then he hid between my front legs and growled.

The people stopped. Then they stepped back—but only a little.

It was like a dream—a horrible nightmare—that would never end. There were scary people and Beep-beep Monsters and tractors and . . . and . . . I'd prob-ably never see my mother again . . . and I missed her so . . . and I wanted to be home in the woods where it was safe and where I belonged . . . and . . .

"HRONK! HRONK!" Booming from beyond the wall of people that surrounded us came the loudest sound I had ever heard.

"Hronk!" I squeaked back. My head jerked as I spun to see where the sound had come from. Mother? It had to be Mother!

The people turned to look, too. Then, like the wake Mother left in the water when she swam, the people began to part. Wider and wider they scattered, until I could see something at the far end of the road. Tall and proud, it was an enormous animal. It looked like Mother. The face was just as beautiful as hers, only everything on it was much bigger. Near the large ears were treelike things that stuck up in the air, just like Mother had told me Father would have.

"*Hronk!*" I squeaked again.

The huge animal trotted toward us. People ran. Some hid inside the buildings. Others hid behind trees. The ones closest to us climbed up on the flat car with the people who had hard heads. Others crouched behind the giant hooves of the tractor. Some of the people didn't run at all. Not until the powerful animal got close to them. All he did was look and lower his head. They squealed and scampered away.

I felt tiny as the big moose stepped nearer. His huge shadow crossed the road as he walked up to me. I stretched my neck, but I still couldn't see all of him.

With a toss of his head he looked down at me.

"Are you Bub Moose?" His voice seemed to echo against the buildings.

"I . . . I . . . Yes, I'm Bub Moose." Suddenly I began to tremble.

"Bub Moose, your mother has been looking everywhere for you. She was afraid that you were hurt. Where have you been?" His nostrils flared, but his big brown eyes were soft.

"I . . . I'm sorry. I . . . we . . . fell off the cliff, and we've been trying to find the way back up the mountain. I don't know where we have been. We were looking for our mothers. Do you know where our mothers are?" I peered through my long eyelashes at the great moose towering above me.

"Your mother is searching for you in the forest. You have worried her too long. Follow me, now!" The big moose turned and started down the road.

"Who . . . who are you?" My knees felt wobbly as I stepped out.

The magnificent moose turned toward me. "Bub Moose, I am your father. You have caused enough trouble. Let's go!"

"You're my father?" A shiver raced up my spine and made my tail jerk. Mother had told me that someday I would grow up to look like my father. But I was so little and he was so . . . so . . . It was very hard for me to grasp what he had said.

"I am your father. We'll talk about this later. Right now we need to get away from these people. I warned them when I came into town, but they will soon feel brave again and we need to leave. Some of them are already beginning to come back out of their buildings." He turned and walked toward the woods.

"What about Snow?" I asked.

"Snow? What are you talking about?"

"Snow is my friend." I bent and looked between my front legs. Snow wasn't there. I bent more. Looked farther. Snow stood way back, under my tummy, where the giant moose couldn't see him.

"A *WOLF!* What are you doing with a wolf?"

"Mother told me to be afraid of wolves, but Snow is my friend. Mother said that wolves eat little moose, but Snow won't hurt me. We're friends." I looked up at Father.

Snow crawled out from his hiding place. "I'm Snow. I would never hurt Bub or any other moose for that matter. We have been looking for our mothers together."

"Oh, so that's what all the howling was about last night. You've been missing, too. No wonder the pack was making such a fuss. I guess that you will have to come along. The people are ready to go back to their fun, and a little wolf might not be safe. Let's go!"

Lined up near their buildings, people stood back as we made a small parade into the forest. Father tossed his head occasionally to tell the people that we were just visiting. Snow trotted behind me, his nose high, but his tail was tucked. I tried to see everything all at once. I wanted to remember what people were really like. Mother would want to know that they weren't as horrible as she thought. Weird, yes. But not horrible.

* * *

Father led us away. Everywhere we went, people stared at us. Most of them hid behind trees or were tucked in beside buildings. As we approached, people scattered in front of us. Father let out loud snorts, and we walked on. When someone came close, Father stamped his foot and the people scampered. He held his head high and proud. My head bobbed back and forth as I looked around at all of the excitement. Snow kept his nose close to the ground and his tail tucked behind him.

"Are we ever going to get away from these people?" Snow asked. He seemed nervous and tired.

"Help me remember everything. I want Mother to know each little bit about this. She thinks that people are all bad. I want to tell her about what we saw and did." I glanced back at the little wolf.

"Are you sure that your father knows his way out of here?" Snow glanced back at the people who closed in behind us.

"I don't know. I have never even seen him before. He looks like Mother, only bigger. Mother told me that he would have branches on his head." I stared at the back of the big moose in front of me.

"Silly! Those aren't branches on his head. Those are antlers." Snow's tail flipped back and forth.

"How do you know all these things about people and animals and stuff?" I let out a little snort.

"I try to pay attention to everything around me. Most times I keep my ears perked and my eyes alert. Most of all, I listen to what the others in my pack say. They have been here longer than I have, and they know lots more stuff than I do." Snow's ears were high and pointed.

I perked my ears up, too. We were almost to the safety of the trees and away from the people. Father led us along a ledge at the bottom of the mountain. It seemed like a long time, but he finally found a narrow path that led us toward the top.

Father's big hooves were steady on the trail. My feet slipped and skidded on the loose rocks. I staggered and stumbled several times, trying to stay up. Snow followed farther behind, to keep from getting gravel and pebbles in his face.

When we finally reached a flat open area, my legs were shaky and weak.

Father raised his big head toward the sky. He let out the loudest sound I ever heard.

"HRONK!"

The call was so loud it made my ears flatten against my neck. Then another noise came. I turned toward a tall stand of aspen, listening. There was a commotion. Then the best sound I ever heard filled the mountain air.

"Hronk! Hronk!"

"Hronk!" I squeaked. My eyes darted to the edge of the forest.

"MOTHER?"

I leaped forward, then skidded to a stop. I had to be sure that it was really her.

"Bub Moose! Come here!" My mother stood at the edge of the aspens.

Fast as I could, I bolted to her side. Nuzzling her flank, I found her warm milk. For the first time in a long long while, I felt safe and warm.

Standing tall and proud, Father watched us. After a while, he lowered his head and wobbled his antlers. "I need to go," he said. "Bull moose roam by ourselves. Bub, you mind your mother and don't make us have to come looking for you again."

I nodded, but I didn't let go of my milk.

When Father turned to go, I heard a loud squeaking sound. He didn't step on Snow, but I guess my friend thought he was going to. The little wolf darted behind a dead stump to hide. Father just rolled his eyes and shook his head. He moved off toward the forest.

Suddenly Father stopped. Still and motionless as a mighty fir tree on a windless day, he stood. Then . . . ever so slowly . . . he began to back toward us. Mother stomped her foot, telling me to stop eating breakfast. I stood beside her, listening. All at once she turned.

Now I was between the two giant animals. Mother's rump was on one side and Father's was on the other—with me in between.

I couldn't see anything. I couldn't hear anything. They sure were acting strange, though.

"What is it?" I wondered. "What's going on?"

They both shushed me.

I never saw what they were looking at. Not at first. I *did hear* the growl. It was low and soft at first. Then it came from another direction and yet another. Finally I realized it wasn't one growl, but a whole bunch. They came from all around us, growing louder and more frightening with the passing of each second.

"Leave our baby alone!" Mother and Father warned.

"What have you done with *my* baby?" one of the growls answered back. "Have you hurt him? If you've harmed him in any way . . . we'll have you and your baby for supper."

"Get back!" Father snorted.

"Give me my baby!" A voice snarled back.

I finally saw where the scary growls were coming from.

Wolves!

They moved into the open. They were everywhere. They surrounded us. There must have been a hundred of them. No, a thousand. (Okay . . . well, maybe there were six or seven.)

They appeared from behind the trees and rocks. Their fur was ridged up on their necks and backs. They curled their lips and showed their long white glistening fangs. They moved toward us. Closer and closer and . . .

"All right. You guys knock it off."

Suddenly Snow hopped to the top of the dead stump where he hid. He made the hair on his back bristle up, too. Little as he was, he tried to look mean and brave.

"They didn't hurt me," he said, gnashing his teeth. "Bub Moose is my friend. We were playing, and we got lost. The daddy moose saved us and brought us back to the forest."

"Yeah," I agreed, nudging Father's rump with my nose. "Snow is my friend. There's no need for everybody to get in such a fuss. We're both safe. Nobody's hurt."

A gray wolf moved slowly toward us.

"Snow, you come here. Right now!"

Snow hopped down from the stump and ran to the big wolf. Ears flattened against his head. His tail wagged back and forth as fast as an aspen leaf wiggles in a strong wind. He circled her.

Still glaring at my mother and father, the gray wolf sniffed Snow and kissed him on the forehead. Then . . . she growled at him.

"I warned you about moose. Let's go. You must promise me *never* . . . and I mean, **NEVER** . . . get near a moose again."

Mother flipped her tail. When she did, it clunked me on the head.

"That goes for you, too, Bub Moose," she whispered. "You must never go near wolves again. Promise?"

Snow looked at his mother. I looked at my mother. And . . . at the very same instant . . . we both said:

"I promise."

But when Snow and his pack moved away into the darkness of the forest, he glanced back at me. Snow wagged his tail and winked.

I winked back.

About the Authors

CAROL WALLACE and BILL WALLACE live west of Chickasha, Oklahoma, far from the home of Bub Moose. Years ago, on a trip to the Whiskey Basin Wilderness area in Wyoming, Bill came face-to-face with a baby moose. When he and Carol traveled to Montana, they enjoyed the tales that the residents had of moose encounters. Carol was fascinated and hoped to get only a glimpse of one of the gigantic creatures. They went home without spotting a single moose.

Shortly after the trip, Carol and their daughter, Nikki, decided to go on a "moose hunt" in Oklahoma. The end result was just the beginning of Nikki's special moose collection, as well as the inspiration for this story.

Mush, one of the family's six dogs, served as the model for Snow